Mirror and water gazing

Mirror and water gazing

Kelwyn Sole

POETRY
Gecko

Published by Gecko Poetry
an imprint of University of Natal Press
Private Bag X01, Scottsville 3209
South Africa

© Kelwyn Sole 2001

ISBN 0 86980 996 2

Cover illustration detail from 'Abduction of the Text: Total Eclipse'
by Sandile Zulu
Cover design by Welma Odendaal
Layout by Lesley Lewis, Inkspots, Durban
Printed and bound by Interpak Books, Pietermaritzburg

Some of these poems have been published, in earlier form, in *Academic Worker, Atlanta Review, Bleksem, Carapace, Debate, Illuminations, Isibongo, Kultur/Sprache/Macht, Litspeak, New Coin, The Heart in Exile* and *Ygdrasil*.

Quotations from the following sources are acknowledged:
Colleen Crawford Cousins 'Interview: Joan Metelerkamp' *New Coin* 28 (2) 1992; Antonio Machado *Selected Poems* transl. Alan Trueblood (Harvard University Press, Cambridge Mass., 1982); Archibald MacLeish *Collected Poems, 1917–1982* (Houghton Mifflin, Boston, 1985); Robert Palmer 'Beauty is a Rare Thing: The Ornette Coleman Quartet's Complete Atlantic Recordings' (liner notes to *Beauty is a Rare Thing* (Rhino/Atlantic R2 71410)); Kim Stanley Robinson *Red Mars* (HarperCollins, London, 1992); Theodore Roethke *The Collected Poems of Theodore Roethke* (Anchor, New York, 1975); Arundhati Roy *The Cost of Living* (Random House, New York, 1999); Leslie Swartz and Gerard Drennan 'The Cultural Construction of Healing in the Truth and Reconciliation Commission: implications for mental health practice' *Ethnicity & Health* 5 (3/4) 2000. 'Mirror and water gazing' is a track from Cecil Taylor's *For Olim* (Soul Note 121 150–2).

... the earth itself is in space;
it's just a matter of looking
up and looking down.

— Ornette Coleman

The gull's image and the gull
Meet upon the water.

— Archibald MacLeish

But seek out the other in your mirror,
the other who keeps you company.

— Antonio Machado

i. m. George Alexander Sole (1912–98)

a genealogy in spring

that instant
never held
between dream
and waking
it comes
on me:

the cuckoo's grief

Contents

I
The dream of the blind child   13
Highveld   15
Botchwork   17

II
Three weary portraits   21
            Shopping for Love
            Flights of Fancy
            An Index of her Days
The passionate pilgrims   28
Two nudes, descending a staircase   30
The dream of the President's pander   36
Weather turning   39

III
Deconstruction   45
Lost City   48
Africa my postmodernist beginning   49
Networks   52
Our fathers flirt with war   61

IV
Mugging the rainbow (Notes towards a national anthem)   65
World Bank   68
Also known as   70
This is not autumn   72
To heal the nation   75

The land   79
Slouching towards Bethlehem   80
Our new 'Red Flag'   82
Multiple choice   85

V
Wilderness   89
Tsitsikamma   90
Akkedisbergpas   92
Holiday   94
Glasswork   100
I live in a house   101

VI
Old flames   105
Coitus   111
I like   112
Your smile is a sudden bird   115
Stonework   118

VII
Death of a poet   121
The betrayal of narrative   122
Black lizard on a white rock   125
The crossing   126
The slow war of the flea   128

VIII
The dream of the cricket   133
The undergrowth   135
The dream of the amnesic gatekeeper   137

I

The dream of the blind child

1

born in the wrong body
to festivals of light
this can't be all, i thought –

my father is a lurching noise,
a horizon strangling in;
the chapped promptings
of two calloused hands
that designate my skin

my mother
a muffled space
curled around the belly
of her loss, a deweyed baby
not like me
imagined deep within

my mother fries i am not sated
rain pours my head is always chilled
the door sticks i learn an entrance
a person in the street screams i
am no hiding place

for i am an island of lonely
washed on all sides by brothers and sisters
as they bicker as they laugh

if i drown

2

i try to escape this shadow me

incessant pressing   : to talk to someone
of zinc or mud or plastic   : not born inside a shack
inwards at my palms   : tell me do you exist
              to look for a maybe is it a voice
      i can call my face towards

the things you try to name
frighten me
          can you prove
there is a world that will stay still
so I may know What's Here
              this shaping
that for me can't last but slips
off the tip of finger
after finger

are you another anyone

do you taste of colours

how far must i come forward
to touch you

Highveld

Near a train siding – flanked only
by rust and a palpitance of swifts wheeling
in the dusk – where lancelets of grass
lower their heads and slowly blanch
as winter moons about, but will not go –
there is a place i love –

where once there was something like
a tree – its name the wag-'n-bietjie
– until we called it firewood
so now all i can offer you
are days of dongas irked by wind – my earth

a place with no tall shade or succour

here i try to conjure delight – and love –
through an inkling that there is – a calling
that approximates the barbed wire voice
of the shrike scratching intermittently
across a hesitation of undergrowth
and taunting every vision –

i know there are stories just begun
of things that need to be done
with singing – something
a scrawny tongue of hope perhaps
craving to lap from mouth to mouth
as the light flickers – totters –

the children who will breathe these songs
may one day stand and stare
across the cracked scrolls of this land –
my people's surpassed fumbling words –

perhaps they will guess here a dream of rivers;
perhaps they will build the sea with their minds.

Botchwork

Not enough to be alive,
not enough to read books. A moon

stabs you at a certain angle, at dusk,
in any field you can construe: or

sun stakes you to the ground
in its many declensions. Whatever happens,

you are not there to see it, as you tiptoe
unambushed to the edge of your tongue

but never leap. Only words, diving
like shot ducks into false meanings –

you have no neighbour, you are no
friend, because you cannot clearly

speak. What will it take
to spell this out for you?

II

Three weary portraits

1. Shopping for Love

You can no longer
solve anything, she said,
and fell at length into my arms

in a night fiercely cold and dark
as unused coal: her bed
rendered calcareous by neon:
where I myself
could never rest.

I would have died
to hear her say
I love you.
Long ago,
I tried everything.

Insulted her politics.
Spoke in portencies and riddles.
Groaned on top of her moving
up and down, she like
a flung rug chafing breath
laid beneath me

forehead an alabaster cup
from which I drank, lips pressed,
smelling her whiteness,
smelling no order
to what I thought.

Maybe I can love you but don't put
that thing in me without a condom.

I still can't name her
without rehearsing anger.
– Last night I closed
a hapless lizard into two pieces
with the snap of a window hasp
at the memory of her quirking
and inch-slow smile.

Her body has yawned wide
three times since then
with all the love
she has ejected
into the world,
                           tiny packages

of bliss, miniscule
consumers already ravenous
for birthday presents
and solicited affection,
firecrackers of flesh
latent with spite and carelessness.

I know this is a difficult thing
for an egotist to hear

– you just don't matter *to me.*

Now her husband follows her
around the supermarket
with a basketful of umbrages.

2. *Flights of Fancy*

TV on all day she doesn't watch
a child miming being educated
the panes quiver in anticipation
late afternoon of storms

her first and last home she
can't forget the man did she
sleep with him or who was it
disappeared long ago

it is then she first notices
above a kitchensink that breeds
steelbabies knives forks spoons
outside the birds

have stopped
their aimless badgering for seed
across the struggling sere lawn
begin to congregate

their noise or is it
music over the neighbour's fence
she shuts her ears the familiar
sounds gone now

small doves
mossies forerunners of listen
larger pinions collide with branches
and the – clasp! –

of clawed feet
talons flexed and mustered
her soup has gone cold she must
not lie awake tonight

the sky grown full
of wings it thunders eddies
the birds are closer they circle
fling themselves

against the fanlight
how long will this last how
a tiny crack another dawdles
across glass

her vision she must
sleep she will sleep burrowing
pillow over eyes
                      she dreams
that feathers choke her

3. An Index of her Days

A calligraphy of bamboo
prickling against the sky
a beckoning blue hollow

where we squatted, you and I,
watching turd-fattened brown
crabs issue forth from sewer pipes

at that end of Emmarentia Dam
no one but us would go.

I was not in love.

You were, but not with me,

blonde hair plastered
awry on hollowed cheeks
a dried lustreless straw
static with electricity
as your head wagged
with your embarrassment,
wrists and ankles
thin as paper
fixing the scrawled
need in your eyes

which knew
              your body
had begun to utter
the vacated spaces
of anorexia.

In those days we all said
love was free
              but so,
you'd found, was pain.

        Every morning
you would come, wait
short of breath on the stoep
outside my mother's house

to walk with me
into that gentler country
just around the corner
where children played
among canoeists dogs
dagga smokers paedophiles
pretending not to notice

as you squatted down
and anointed the grass
with a yellow dribble
of your urine,

all the time
trying to find the equipoise
your mouth might not talk away
through your terror you'd go home
to find again

your boyfriend lying
on your bed to lie upon
the hash-smoking heiress
he'd discovered
                    behind
her calves and nipples
clothed
          no longer
in carefully torn denim.

There was no effacement
could cure you quite of him,
despite the prayers you breathed
to a mothering earth
I swear you'd come
to float above –

till I too

fled from your spew of words,
the voiding mutter of self-pity,
the trapped logic
of your flesh.

Now all your time
has gone, and your friends'
postures and bellies
sag down
        but you

always will remain
the force-fed nineteen
years you were the sunrise
that your body died.

Susan, forgive me
this intrusion into
your considered surrender –

trying to sketch the thin
contours of a life;
trying to keep
your small grave clean.

The passionate pilgrims

1

Travelling means nothing to us:
the roads that spoke away from the hub
of our eyes no longer lead

to other cities, only here.
No one spins the wheel.

2

Morning sun renews our faces

with the warm fecal smell of a baby
not quite awake, in the next room:
brings limbs into motion, the same

watches repeating, disembodied voices
on a battered radio. Brings
the pleated songs of car seat covers

at war with coca cola pleading.

3

In this room where we are are
books, rising damp on walls, bland

ishments touching lips, your glans, the place
where the juices of desire
                    flow out
from our bodies, into the sheets, away.

A shower of asteroids
                sperm
scrabbles against the stretched wall
of rubber
            that's its final universe.

4

At night outside when we can see
no longer the line of washing thrums,
hangs out a dead lizard, and a crab.

My fingers tighten closer to your heart.

Two nudes, descending a staircase

1

She comes to him resolutely
without shame,
                    the coffee
still warm and tart
in the back of her throat
brewed by her husband
earlier this morning.

He does not comprehend
her belly crisscrossed with scars
left by departing children;
only the breath flirting
up to winter,
her breasts insistent
against the jersey's thick wool
her body has arrived in

tense with anticipation
in honour of them,
who became.

2

So much space
to feel anxious
in this city of wide
roads and rows
of matching
house facades
that hides them
without complaint

                     – a face withdrawn
behind thick curtains
                     – the furtive slipping
of someone's blouse through
the stucco of a gateway,
where shadows crumple
in a happenstance of sunlight.

They inhabit a domain
made up of the four lips
they fare across
to knowledge of each other

the bridge

of their crossing
as they shout release
                     as if
they wished the world to hear

a bridge

which dangles them
above a handful of minutes
in which they slake their thirst.

    3

Yet there is also
no place for her:
he is dazed by his
bitter self-fulfillment
a profile a good name
he wishes he could lose

their ambush
into gentleness
        a presentiment
that their shoes' laces have been tied
to the pavement long before

so they cannot run
further away or closer;
only tread the same spot,
crippled by the placement
of their dissembling.

    4

Thinking of him though she finds
she cannot close her windows
even at night

but her arms are filled
with the certainties of loving,
a man a son two daughters,
her heart a placid habit
in rhythm with their promptings.
Only her dozing nipples
rise up in dreams like coral
tips break the meniscus
of the sheets
of the room
of the home
of the suburb
where she abides

desire she can't fathom.

5

To be taciturn
when he wants to yell
a profane tenderness

from the green tower
of the mosque which suppliant
pleads with God five times
a day
        from the prim bells
of churches he has long vacated
                    from the ancient
drums the clapping hands in rapture
the consonance of *tefillim*
through which her fathers disapprove

all fading into distance.

Now he prays for nothing more
than those brief hours
he can close his door

and place his ear
between her legs.

6

There is no balance   to sustain them
a fumbling of zippers   and buttons
that burgeons to bare flesh   intermittently
frenzied with hope   and craving

capricious as a rockface crannied with earth
carping at its sudden flowers

as he acrobats with precision
past the wife expectant
to catch him   and she changes
direction   in midair

improbable dives
between disaster and delight
depending on each other,
the capture by love's fingertips.

    7

Reforming whole again
into the piecemeal of their skin

                    she feels
her own sense of touch renew
and start to itch,
          his heart
to race with magic and
with wonder

         though ulcers
can still stitch
a usual modicum of pain
under their ribs —

    8

coming to ardour
late in life is irremediable,
when flesh no longer goes
towards its reconnoitring
with any doctrine of belief
to marshal into earnestness
behind it. O they know:

there have been other rooms
on other quiet afternoons
they separately have watched
                          a face
much like his or hers
muscle into the relentless pillow light
of an awakening.

They will never decide
why this feels so different.

The dream of the President's pander

How many years must I watch him
abuse the opened legs of women
with his poetry and cocksureness,
his half-attention?

I've always made this space
        for myself, he'll say,
breathing garlic and that faint
        middle-aged
stench of decay, leaning in
rubbing his drooping belly
into the curls of each one's hair,
the hard bone above the pubis.

Her mouth can never answer,
choked full as it becomes
with that pink head of muscle,
followed by the seed of power

drying upon the quilt.

This is when I pity her,
when she still supposes he
will find the time to cherish her

as the night rides, an olive in a glass
knocking on the aftertaste of dreams,
the credulity he tips up and gulps down,
one body upon another.

But still
it's me who buys him his cigars,
watches entranced at a one-way mirror
as he thrills to slowly force them
up each vagina.

    *   *   *   *

I've seen the trust
of every woman used
and then scrubbed out,
tumbling down beyond
his cajolery his assurances
and grapplings of routine
towards a too-brief reverie
where she can be (not on her back,
at last) herself.

I've seen his grimace and jerk
of ecstasy too many times,
the flop back to an appointed face
where there is no empathy,
only the loll of glutted matter
feeding upon silence.

Today there is a steady weeping
under my skin,
a spirit I have never borne,
a weight that is my self disconsolate
condensed around his whims,
his mirror of calculations,
his gaze

dazzled by her replicas.

    *   *   *   *

I have lied and offered love
to those who prowl the fretful streets
of their need for tenderness
: am their betrayer

and can only,
into the mute aftermath,
concoct a shout –

the pupa of love
prickling still
born beneath my flesh.

Weather turning

1

From reclaimed seasand
– a hidden corner of his garden –
among tangles of fennel,
of sour fig and fuschias,
the mouldering forepaws of a mole
he once broke with a spade

                        peep

in yellow twigs
               that cannot bloom.

His anger at its depredations
is forgiven now. The sun holds him
to this noon like an old scar.

2

Yarrow blooms neglected
in her yard: red, white and yellow
in pinpricks of tiny blossoms
pinpricks of light: seeming

to duck even while rooted
the starlings jitterbugging across
to strip its leaves this spring
for their soft birthings, or puff
out its tiny chests of perfume
at bees which drone past
unheeding,
intent
       on the more pungent lure
of basil, thyme or hyssop.

3

This is where farmers
once raised potatoes,
never used clever words
to note the world they knew.
They are absent but to hearsay.

Even the term their workers
gave the place – Sjambokland –
has been throttled
under the dust of many summers.
The fitful vleis have been drained.
Cans and bottles wink like eyes
on a remaining hint of water

while front-end loaders
level the earth for new fields and houses
to stage sport or domestic quarrels.
One last black-necked heron parades
for mice across the fresh-laid turf:
crushed mole snakes blazoned
on the highway.

4

Nothing to do,
she nibbles at an orange,
imagines the hands plucking it
still rank upon its skin, peels
to where the juice is tart;
rubs withered shanks together.

She is too shy
to stand in her stained apron
where she might be noticed

comes out only later
in the dusk
to skitter and twirl her thoughts
across the heads of kattekrui and buchu.

5

And he plods

through restraining mandibles
of grass
        to his fire-tinged border
the picket fence over which
a bouganvillea pants incessantly
in stubborn tongues of purple
bereft in a wrong assumption
of the season

starts to clean away
the cigarettes and wrappings
from his last encounter
with his loud-voiced son
and daughter

– is there life beyond their cell
phones their unit trusts
their constantly vocalised opinions?
If his wife could see them now! –

and dig
the sacrificed shadow
spreading out from his toes
to make new beds for seedlings,

building for birdsong,

waiting to lift his eyes anew.

And if the pelican should pass
over the roof, sagging and begrimed,
of his house he will breathe in
breathe out in out with wonder.

6

The spider will get trapped in its web;
the fly no longer die forgetful;
dropping its murderous insinuations
the feather duster will wilt on its hook;
and her ceiling also glow
its marginal, remembered white.

7

Is that enough to know

enclosed in their gardens, listening
over the walls, watching
the sky, without glasses
            without focus

with no means to glance
across all this greenness
                    and see
the exact moment

the weather could start to turn.

III

Deconstruction

He runs everywhere everywhere along the planes of identity
as they shift, each
realm of darkness chasing its Other:

has flitted over rocks, past caves,
through fields of endless screeds
bristling their sprigs of intention

… he reads, his eye follows, his eye is a moon
lurching towards what is outside
                                        through mutations
of what's been written

– this text, he says, illuminates

            *   *   *   *

composed in some study
on our behalf
he
                first-world academic
moulting nightly onto his desk
                                        an unsprightly parakeet

while the beauties of a New England Fall
surround him

pursues the trace of a breath
left by the harsh-throated wolf of meaning

panting its stink always
just slightly out of reach

trails its ever-receding spoor
across pages of delightfully
scripted, subversive

paper

*   *   *   *

once or twice
he has allowed us (by good grace of himself)
the authority
to dream
            granted us
remote beings
threatened exalted
by less harmless
rebellions
than his own

            a future
where equality and justice
have their inkling

though always (*in the last instance*) he
can't help it, he, regretfully
arrogates the power
to scratch the incitement *truth*
off our graves our flags
                        as if
it were a swearword

*   *   *   *

for him

there will always be new boundaries
to be imagined
trespassed
uttered across

but for us

there are only these boundaries
marking us   the edges of
our goat-destroyed landscapes
of our expungable skins

the necessity
of touch all we have
                to give in love
                or brutality

beyond which we
                cannot reach
because of which we
                can't transcend
the provincial unglamour of

our lives, these deaths

Lost City

Imaginary beings, in a real landscape.
— *Kim Stanley Robinson*

By the Kong Gates we paused
                    but could not think
beyond the icons the vistas
given to us unfolded. Two plaster parrots
betrayed our trust
                    and would not move. We traipsed
through baobabs, rain forest, a desert
past exotic llamas — a world in one country —
interrupting no creature of breath. Latex rocks groaned
beneath our hard heels, and an electric cable
                    whipped by the breeze
hissed.
                    At the Valley of Courage
there was only the splat and slurry of piped water
awaiting us playmates
                    and our fall.

All our cities are lost. By
the one-armed bandits
we hunker down,
and forget to weep.

Africa my postmodernist beginning

for Lesego

1

africa
my beginning

in the middle
of the life
of my journey
a tourist

between commas
searching, never
searching for
the should of
closure my ending

africa my in
spiration (the
people)
       their
presence here
as absences
enunciations they
interject through
resistant hearts

when one's
not looking

2

my other
mother

the sky trembles
with infinite
clouds I see
horizons always
l
 i
  m
    i
    n
   a
 l
ly as master
narratives settle on
the advertisements for
my people
            commodities and clocks
light up their
lost their
hungry eyes

3

primal voices
i pine for
at each
crossroads i safari
through
            in my mind
my participles
all still
dang
      lin
          g

i the interpreter
delete that
the facilitator
of interpretations

transcendentally
imperative

as I process words
in this suburban room

outside history

4

but africa
my lines are
all metonymies
are impis
now at war
                    are

hybrid timebombs
ticking

5

my endless
writings
of beginnings
in this sentence
of writing
endlessly *my africa*

6

the end

Networks

1

The Dandenongs
heaving hazy with heat out of the morning
        jumpy as fleas in relentless sun
                are if you get nearer
        only a green gullet

of gum trees and belling birds
        that swallows ferns, roads,
                a snake or two, gang-gang cockatoos
        blackened tree stumps as well
                as children's burnt-out toys
                        from last year's
        fire. Behind tangling wire fences
                with rusted gates awry
                        creak the lorn fates of houses.

Here, late summer rumples the suburbs into a doze
                that defies all efforts
        to pinpoint ardour for a task
                larger than hospitality
        or making babies, to find a way
to choose or understand.

The cumulus that sails above these hills
        inexorably east to west also pends its promise
                above my mother's backyard
        clouds of rain or clouds of washing.
She is slackened by the weight of nine decades
                that seem to her in retrospect
        continuously parched.

The area is mistakable – it could be anywhere
           architects and builders conspire
           through a gagging of dust and effort
           to make walls that will keep
           us out, or in –

but my mother is displaced. Her South African
gutturals sharpen more completely into tiny stones
each year, inflect upwards into her nose with a tang
           of fire and eucalyptus
           she can't control, and
           no longer even ascertain.

Cinched in a green belt under signposts
to Elm Crescent and Dominion Avenue
she waits to die. Her descendants
have all gone native, except
the unruly son who stayed behind where
she was born to contest against her – his –
           race. Alone, she watches
           the wattle birds in pairs

twirl upside down and prod
inside the banksias, irate clowns.
I don't know but these days
I think there are parts of me
not properly connected to the world.
           She dreads the obstinacy
           of aging joints, her fading

sight, the thought that she
may someday need my charity.
Women with big hams cheeriness
and sympathy who bring her
charcoaled chips 'n chicken
           are all the human warmth
           she finds. And what if
           she should falter? Where

on earth would I be?

2

In a basement apartment in
Greenwich Village

                  where mould
erects fetid green sepals
insistent as cheese.
               I try
to sleep, but the curtains are
too short, and a chaos of legs
toting disembodied laughter pass
procure a night of sleeplessness
− *what does it do for you to say*
such shitawful things to me?
− *Charlie, don't be like that!*
− *where's that ugly-assed mother?*
− *been to The Mummy? It's great! −*
Man, I'm telling you … − por Dios!
− *that's the biggest rat I've ever seen!*
− *you lost?*
                come up to the sidewalk
owl-blinking in a morning light
that glares and treacles
through fire escapes
and railings
to fret

on brownstone
a latticework
of etched ebony
shadow. Yellow
cabs in the streets
swerve and drone
like hornets
                till
                pinched between
unscalable cliffs of commerce
the sun fulfils its moment,
flounders, then
                        is gone. Swarms
of faces on the street interweave
jokes and imprecations

servants of the Web –
that galaxy of disconnected facts
that's centred here but nowhere,
the lure to shop and never stop
spidering across the globe.

Along the East River
the fantasy of equal kinship
among all nations maunders
in an insoluble brisk wind

as pages from torn-up speeches
careen across the plaza. Flags
nod their heads, then lunge
out in impotence …

3

1st May. Dear Robert: I have come home,
but not without a troubled heart.

Their cities are much like ours, but strive
to be bigger and more daunting.

They claim to have rubbed out lack and anger
but I saw white packets circulate in alleys

and people cry out with no hope at all
in the early morning streets of their pain.

Still, they have one or two endearing habits —
e.g. they pretend to listen when you speak.

But they grow nonchalant with a glut of choices.
Believe to carry guns everywhere helps them

find a liberty. And worse, still kill (not as we,
fear blade-borne and with recklessness of hunger)

but by injecting their pariahs with toxin
then pretending they are just asleep.

I meandered. And — call this ridiculous —
in all places I heard ghostplaints hang

in the concrete nooks and crannies
of their spring:
                    May Day. Mayday.

4

As for me, returned

a day without largesse —
the sun's declining power
alone gives to me,
in my own country,
a tourist's scrimped
interlude of happiness,
the mountain splintering

into lines of pure form.

Sunday brings a chilled wind
gesticulating towards autumn:
a cold front heaps at the horizon
sheared off into cobalt on its top
as if by a lathe. But we've waited
all week for this, hulking down
in offices in homes on wastelands
of gaunt inner-city desolation
balanced on the tightrope humdrum
of construction sites or
office chairs
                and now
it's come — a half-day of shopping
followed by empty hours
when there's no need to ponder
or to move

even though
somewhere close by
a stone takes out the eye
of a taxi driver riding past
at the wrong place and time
steel proves the truism
once again that it is
more durable than flesh
and the stench of the refinery
sinks its claws repeatedly
into the sinuses of children

but the brewery fumes also
a sweet piss smell of languor;
there is a repeated drowsy click
as bat belabours ball through which
I dream away the afternoon

wake up once more
into a disgrace of motives
coming to seed coming to blight,
the talking heads of those
once mistaken as my comrades
now academics consultants bankers
clowns who juggle interest rates
spindoctors of The Market —
the bumbling chimeras of our age
excusers of the growing debt
we owe to foreign systems

who twinkle now on now off
of the persistent screens
of allurement in our homes,
and regulate our harvests.

5

Tomorrow a diligence of noise
will rivet the air.

         A fortuitous
small house next door
seeks its shape
accreting bricks each day
– saws and hammers
                not quite
in unison –

       human beings
at work probing
for new beginnings
          shelters

someone may come to call
their own,
      a future
of good neighbours

we'll hope one day
to feel secure
enough to

consummate.

6

Feel your tongue
bestir itself
        with the strain to articulate –
        years that crackle like tinder –
unstoppable wish
        that someday
the furious songs
        of incorrection
and incorrigibility
might threaten
        with our deeds.

No one should be content
merely to declaim
        that the worst poverty
is a lack of reference,
a looking always
        somewhere else:

but it is
the first
        mortifying,
            necessary
                step –

Melbourne – New York – Cape Town

Our fathers flirt with war

The doors which were shut
were opened
to let us glimpse
a few uncertain profiles
peering out, like indistinct artichokes.

It was then I first saw you.

But now the fragile sky
teeters above,
         a plate
full of cirrus-chips. I find

I can no longer wash my hands,
no longer eat without your mouth.

There is a cracking sound
as we separate one from the other
         as if we were
children called home from play,
or old tram lines uncoupling.

Locks are being bolted
with the keys of suspicion
up and down the street.
The doors which were opened
are being shut again,

and your face
will fade quickly
from recall.

IV

Mugging the rainbow
(Notes towards a national anthem)

Found poems

We're not using celebrities
because they're celebrities.
We're using them because
they reflect the average person.

* * *

Fashion, like history, repeats itself.

* * *

We've come to kill the police
because
they are fighting with us
although
we are not fighting.

* * *

I simply
picked it up and
pulled the trigger

each time I wanted
to shoot. From that day,
I became

a graduate in shooting.

* * *

This is my favourite mini. Unfortunately
I only wear it out at
funerals. So you don't see it
as often as I'd like you to.

* * *

Our decisions are always people-driven.
When in doubt, we consult our lower organs.

* * *

A country with a
humane, caring prison system

will have a
humane, caring society.

* * *

There is pessimism and the view
that crime is escalating.

This is simply not true.

If murder statistics are taken,
almost 90 percent of them
are committed by relatives
and poor people. But
still there is

this pessimism about crime.

* * *

You can't argue
with the whites.
They say
     always
it was the computer.

* * *

You've got to reveal,
not expose;
you know what I'm saying?

* * *

You know, we really
didn't have much information.

But we didn't need any.

* * *

I'm showing
my most soft,
my most erogenous
zones —
     I've got some traditional stuff, too,
because, you know, I'm
from the Eastern Cape,
          and *that's*
where tradition's all happening.

* * *

It was simply a photo opportunity.
Nothing serious was discussed.

World Bank

1

A mood of dancing
of celebration
fills the air.

Praise singers update their names,
dreadlock their hair –
make certain
camera lenses target
their fervour and
their tonsils
            bobbling
from one take to the next
in front of baobab trees
made up from paper-maché.

Everyone patterns
their physiques with chevrons
with dyed cloth edged in swahili
with day-glo ndebele patterns

and free t-shirts
entwining arms black and white
fists tilting
viva beer

– there is a constant hubbub
of wrangling convictions
and coins in concert.

2

       What
an agony of futures it is
at last to hope!
         To pound
the earth's rubble
importunate tearing
at our heels
as if the expelled blood
everywhere we step

in this landscape of sharp edges

no longer laid claim
to the terse seepage
of anger
       our hearts
have clenched into.

3

To prophesy the cost
  of all this
would need clear vision
        not this dust
        not this dust
we've raised ourselves

would need
an art to watch
carefully the entrances the exits
to the foreign embassies –

to see beyond those
welcoming bright blossoms
in front of their high walls.

Also known as

As they disinter your bones
there is no speech can extol you.
Like brittle stalks of flowers
they emerge, one by one,
followed at last by the dry pod
that had housed your brain:
you, fighter against injustice,
bearer of the dreams of multitudes.
And a lot of people stand
here by your graveside,
and call you hero: one or two
you might have known,
when they visited you in training
among the dust and thorns and flies
from their *important work*
in Stockholm or New York.

Every time they fossick
round to find the grave
of those like you
who died by torture
or the ranting of a bullet
there are bouquets, and perorations,
and balloons to fly above the place
from which a sleep is broken

although occasionally
they dig the wrong bones
and find not you the hero but
the rest of us lying here,
the carpenter all thumbs,
the dealer in batteries and coal,

the pimp, the mechanic
whose backyard is filled
with hijacked cars ...
                    and then
there is a lot of confusion;
they take the bunting down;
and the hearses slink off
with the wreaths and anthems,
and leave us,
                    and someone
shovels hasty earth back over us.

So? Is there a tale in this
that can justify its maker?

I know only this. Alive,
I found someone snatched
away that puff of air
forming at my lips each time
I tried to speak:
                    and now still
I'm required to lie here
with their cumbersome shoes
smelling of foot lotion
and Italian leather pressing
down upon my body,
as I carry the dead weight
of a memorial, its verdigris
of memory then forgetting,
and always more dogma,
and always me wanting
to scratch the itch
of the fourth dimension
under my armpit.

I wish they'd go home.

This is not autumn

This is not autumn:
the skies are doused
in aching blue
without respite

nights are colder
there is little cloud
to entice us
into warmth.

Queleas swarm
in flocks like
grasshoppers
no longer

each farm drowses
after its harvest,
and quiet descends
on a veld surrendered

to a seared brown
to crackling scurf
and the slow musk
of wood fires.

We traveled
with belief
on shining roads
to know the lives

of our compatriots,
their heartbeat.
But our own thoughts
change. There is

panic and eagerness loose in the world. Last night's hotel tv was pregnant
with praise singers. You fell asleep, during *education comes through sport*,
and I had no strength to touch the dial to release me from my vigil
alone with shy mice and the maudlin sound of tyres in love with tar.
There was a hint of lightning, a trance of rain, briefly, to the east:
then from the west a sifting in the dewless sand, grain on lonely grain:
from the south a dirge came for the lost herds of Cochoquas:
from the north a tintinnabulation of trumpets and applauding jewelry
as ancient powerful men wagged thick forefingers in admonition
just like those before them.

In Hillbrow the streets are shattered glass.
In Pretoria they mint reflecting coins to spy any threat approaching.
In Orange Farm and Khayelitsha, a furtive noise of bailing buckets.
In Richmond there is no one who dare recognise a neighbour.

Tomorrow we will forfeit ourselves again to the soothings
of clerics, their fantasies of blame and of redemption tricked out
in rainbow colours. Will drive past billboards crooning the idiom
of Herdbuoys and Azaguys. See more of bureaucrats
– a glacial indifference – young people grown slickly self-important
in offices
                vocal with assurances they cannot hope to keep
who find time to redeem their own mortgages
with down-payments of our patience.

                        Yet for now
a woman passes us and waves and can't stop grinning
with the promise of a house – at last – within her eyes.
A child muses, longing for a friend to share his prickling intellect.
An old man reclaims his land, ploughs the soil with the joyful
calloused foresight of all who carry seed. Bricks
seek mortar then resolve to transform themselves to buildings.
Girls in *makgabis* are sinuous hankering for one day love

as we stop in the exact centre of this journey,
a chrome and steel button
                         among mealiefields stubbling in all directions
with no map to tell us where to go
                              – seek anywhere
a language of candour a signpost but are awake only
to the sad shunting of a train, somewhere in the distance;
or try to read a script of looping ants
devouring a sandwich.

There are riddles
that possess us

                        that we fear to name, enraptured
with optimism, yet weighted down with our forefathers'
genetic tombstones still clogged inside our brains.
A plague of eloquence beguiles this world to posturing,
a misplaced sanctimoniousness of spring.
The air stinks of trouble. And myths proliferate.

To heal the nation

Good day, nurse.
– er, molo: I'm
Doctor Voges. This
intern is doing the rounds
with me – her name
is ...

Patient interrupts in Xhosa.

What did he say, Nurse
– Dhyoba? ... no,
don't worry: just tell him
I'm here to help.

Nurse, in Xhosa, to the patient.

So what's the problem?

He wants to go to the TRC:
he wants to go back
to sign papers.

What papers?

Asks, in Xhosa.

Speaks in Xhosa.

He says
he wants release
of the papers regarding his injuries.

Attempts to thank the patient in Xhosa.

> – but sorry, sir:
> also about his expulsion
> from the squatter camp.

From the informal settlement?
Oh, yes … .

Ask him for me:
what does he want
from the TRC?

> *In Xhosa.*
>> *In Xhosa, talking to the nurse.*

> He says
> all the leaders of that time
> should be arrested. He
> has not seen his family
> since 1986.

> *Talks in Xhosa.*
>> *Abruptly in Xhosa.*

What are you two saying?
Arrest the people?
Does he know them all?

> He knows them all.

But we've been through this already with him!

> *In Xhosa.*
>> *Replies in Xhosa.*

> He asked 4 times
> for his documents.
> We haven't given them.

What documents?

In Xhosa.

At length, in Xhosa.

All the documents
taken from him.

In Xhosa.

Murmurs angrily in Xhosa.

Ish!

Berates the patient in Xhosa.

How will they be of any use?

In Xhosa.

Explains in Xhosa.

Astonished, in Xhosa.

What?

Vociferously, in Xhosa.

He says his life story
is there

to verify what he has
been saying and to help
with their arrest.

We can't help him
… the TRC can't arrest
all these people!

Interjects glumly in Xhosa.

Gesticulates impatiently then
speaks in Xhosa.

– The TRC think he is ill.

– Do you want to ask him
any questions, Annelise?

      – not really,
Doctor …

               Shrugs, mutters in Xhosa.

      He says:
      shoot me dead then.

      Remonstrates with the patient in Xhosa.

– Is he
a political authority?

I don't think so.

      He says,
      he has no affiliation:

      he says he wants
      nothing to do with it.

The land

– You see my house.
You see my wife,
my children, my mealies
and my dogs? Yes, over there –
They say I am hiding in this forest.
They say I have gone back
to drinking with the animals.
But in the location I would be
no one. I would just be

that thing that they call unemployed.

Slouching towards Bethlehem

1

The nights are inevitable
and very cold: are bitter
as if the taste of paint

were grained upon their gums.
The rough texture of wasps
slumberous droning with threat

rain slants down. The earth
continues to grind and
groan around its axis.

Some sleep on soft beds,
some on straw and rotting cardboard:
mud is a resting place

as good as any for those
so many who can't recount
a single summer. I am one

in this drizzle of patient eyes.
We watch. We calculate.
Don't ever think we will

allow ourselves to be forsaken.

2

Today was blown feathers for hours
away away from us.

3

A time of reckoning drips off the eaves,
enters the souls of the dinner guests,
despoils their last parties.

The raucous house is still fully lit,
but there are fists there are hands
hoodwinking
                    towards the switches ...

the rain a whimper of rebuke
first hesitates on weary leaves
then thunders again on every roof

— flesh shivers with intent but finds
no body's warmth (love's an itch
ill-scratched by winter).

We wait to be defined
by touch, by reciprocity
are those who seek

a dawn where our blindness
will seem a blessing
                    as
the erudite emerge

brash and fumble-fingered. For
we know
            in the coming century
whose resolve will falter first.

Our new 'Red Flag'

follow the bouncing ball …

The workers' flag's been put to bed
– At least that's what Mokaba said –
The struggle's altered, never fear,
It's time to shift to Mbeki's GEAR.

So lift our Ramaphosas high!
Beneath their shade you'll live and die!
In the rainbow nation all's for sale,
… So in your coffin goes another NAIL.

The SACP (what a joke!)
Went and postponed the workers' yoke;
That stage will come! – meanwhile till then,
Wait for a house in Two-Thousand-Ten.

So wave our tailored suits aloft!
Our kaftans and our kente cloth!
Despite banquets and encomia,
We're still Left when on podia.

The liberals are changing hue
To black and white – you'll be black and blue;
Yes, simunye, now *raise* that fist,
As long as you stay capitalist.

But if our profits should abate,
We can't swear to our interest rate!
The nation's fiscus we hold dear,
But may go offshore by next year.

Your guilt your loss your grief and lies,
Our clergy will redemptionize;
To Godsell hearken, cease to jeer,
Find in your soul the entrepreneur.

Come, carol in the treble clef!
To free trade and the IMF!
We'll gather, meet all stakeholders,
Leave you new pens and SANLAM folders.

We bonga, simper, shake the hands
Of moneyed folk from foreign lands;
Swop Cabral's words for journalese,
"Tell lies, claim easy victories".

Now raise your arms and stomp those feet!
Madiba-jiving's hard to beat!
For Clinton, Arafat and co.,
Our will to please will outlast Nzo.

We're post-Production (*forget* that fist!)
Rails each funky post-modernist;
It's a carnival, now, drop your guard,
Time for aerobics with Lyotard.

So lift aloft your differance*!*
It's good here if it's good in France!
Ideology is gone for good,
And if it's not, well, it really *should!*

Multicultural, now, apartheid-free,
We can rejoice in our history;
Both roots-conscious and non-racial,
Each free to fake our own Hintsa's skull.

So praise the forefathers you find!
Change the dark past to ease your mind!
Give no offence, that's the yardstick;
Our ethnic cleansing's done with Jik.

Our Renaissance is under way,
In Parliament, in Pick 'n Pay,
In spaza shops, in factories,
We must strive to be visionaries.

So follow our pipe-smoking boss,
As he warps and woofs his consensus!
Market trends will change — ignore the rumours —
Quite soon we'll all be blithe consumers.

Multiple choice

White State Black State
                    what State
the thing turns out always the same
pledge your being to their looking-glass
what's left outside the frame?

the local or the global
it couldn't matter less
to consultants on our poverty
who depend for their success

on bedazzling every one of us
each Gita Mpho or Roy
timid
        in our unity of greed
for one more shiny useless toy

we speak no longer heart to heart
media clichés cloak our solitude
we're just sleek graduate tourists now
from their schools of software and fast food

global gangsters cast no shadow
their country's nothing but their style
use up the planet with panache and leave
us each resulting fresh shit pile

they say this bedazzlement can't be broken
that's the fable they want heard
but it can, by partisan activity directed at

– *you* find the next, the magic, word.

V

Wilderness

1

A flock of hadedas —
steam from a distant train —
vlei and forest —

cry achingly as they roost;
whistles tiny silver notes;
pleat in towards evening.

2

The moon,
a wan bystander,
has faltered down behind the trees:

only a nightjar's avowal
still curbs
the dark night.

Tsitsikamma

The first act of forgetfulness
is to enter the silence,
and to drown.

* * *

At your back
the sea's horizon
masses and sufflates clouds

dwindles behind a frame
of undergrowth and bracken

at every glimpse.

* * *

After a few steps
there is a nervous flickering
within the leaves, a jauntiness
of tiny silhouettes
that hop along the branches

mimed beneath your feet,
dancing where the light
sieves down.

Assegai, yellowwood, bladdernut,
`turkey-berry, wild almond, saffron
a profligacy of roots and creepers
witch hazel and num-num
jumble their braids
down the gorges.

The stump of the hard pear
rings like a gong.

* * *

Don't be afraid:

the boomslang will mark its passage
with a susurration of ruffled leaves
that moves away

even as it sinews on and on,
into your imagination.

* * *

After each storm
frogs scatter
tiny bells
of self-affirmation.

A chortle of water
purls down
into pools
russet as dried blood.

* * *

No one
can gainsay

the foot
that plods uphill,

that slips,
but keeps its purpose

no longer
captive to a shadow.

Akkedisbergpas

for Péter Kántor

1

Past the two dimensions
of burnt wheatfields
and a laceration of dongas,
on the edge of stone
toppled high on stone,
a garden

hoists its green surrender.

2

Here
fruit trees squint
lemon and orange
eyes in all directions.

Taste fattens
in regiments.

3

Sopped
in heat

the air
begins

to clot.

4

No sign

of life except
a tiny bird

of wingclaps
bragging its song

and spiralling
a freckle

of sound
next to
      the sun.

Holiday

The edge is what I have.
— Theodore Roethke

I trod that day as
one going barefoot, through
the heavy copper air
of early morning. Desiccated
branches crackled on the path,
and a dappled cock ridiculous
as a handkerchief tattered
by the wind was blown
an optimist to his next meal

came to the main road
to wait among dim figures
swaddled in blankets against the cold
remarking on the house
newly-built across the road.
That place? It's Motlhagodi's.
Most of the year he's in Gauteng.
That's why he's rich. It's said
he'll build a bigger soon, in fact.

And they admired
the pink-daubed walls tin roof
winking its corrugations the bay windows
burglar bars new in their ostentation
on the outskirts of their village.

*   *   *   *

Voices set against
the motor's wheeze and stumble
       the taxi lurched
through plateaux of sand-washed bush
where goats stare with alien eyes
and will not move. In the seats

crammed full of our hopes and us

I talked to the woman next to me,
her face the story of her mother
and her mother's mother: all
the centuries pounding maize
for indifferent men   ending in
her own self-pitying drunken husband
she was now escaping

while those around us
sang, layer upon layer
of flimsy sound, building
out of the heat and the haze
the sweat which trickled off
bodies of tenacity

that told of pain, and need to work,
and land hard lost.

                        In the shadow
of Lobatse we parted, where
the finger of the mosque
is a beckoning that tickles
God. She, on her way
to work for a civil servant as
a servant. I waved
                        to where
                        she waited
                        arms akimbo
                        for a bus
crossed railway tracks —
feet grinding in. the rubble —
then skipped
between two shunting trains.

Five hours later I saw
the town in which my birth
nearly killed my mother peer out
like a pustular concrete toad
between its warts of minedumps.

            *   *   *   *

It was a long holiday.
Jacarandas postured all
around me in streets

breeding weavers
                        sizzled
their inanities at the sky.

I spoke to
the pale children with whom
I had grown up: found the city
changed little   still their monument:
granite statues flaring billboards
high walls razor wire
                              the bland now
multicultured faces of those
who by their love of money

labour on to idolize

a tale of warmongers and heroes
who had sown their bibles maxims
as seeds into the earth. Jo'burg
wears its slums like petticoats,
flaunts best what it tries to hide.

Old friends, I have no hands,
but seek you still –
I salute you, myself,
our mothers and our fathers –
I salute those who never know
those not themselves

who are the mirrors still
determining my face

whose face now (it seems)
finds many ways
to modulate its colour

                *   *   *   *

Look at what
these features wrought

a woman yawls from her stoep,
watches her breasts slump with time.
The room behind her a rustle
of cockroaches, comrades to
the dreams of babies. Long nights
and days of wine and razors

brothers flung together – so close –
they imagine nothing else but how
to eat each other's hearts. Among
dustbins young girls
heave disjointed smiles, then offer
the purse between their thighs.

I think
        of Rosa Luxemburg,
that uncomely woman
of hunchbacked visions
who knew true love, and wonder
at my lack of it,
                wonder at
the beauty of a country come to be
a pawn to lure the gullible with lies,
an icecream on a loaf of bread.

            *   *   *   *

So I left early.
Came back to rest
where I started from

splattered down
among cows and donkeys
and Seventh Day Adventists,
the vacant huts of migrants,
my yearning in stifling shebeens
next to drunken teachers

here where it rains like doomsday
once a year

its green
       a certitude
of more thorns in the future
and little else

but a place where I
am sure I will be greeted
by everyone I meet
each morning

where I find myself simply as
another
               somewhere
at least to live.

Glasswork

the face
as a traveller
through time
has to peer   the face comes
into solidity   a greedy tourist buried
to assure itself   at the bottom
                     of a pond
where the mirror   clear as glass,   in whatever season
          is   evocative of a king   you seek him
he smiles he's human and his madness   who does not change
          is not   his lovely hardness
the distortion   there
          it   rocks back and forth   he dies
is an image   a minute world   he
you know too well   so bland and flat,
yourself   a private Africa   is close
                     with its obsessions   closer than
                     its Occident   your thinking of
                                                      yourself
                     the same   seeking a mystery
                     bogus magic   into which
                     you fall   whatever
                     your pride takes
                     from you   losing

                                            is a dimension

I live in a house

I live in a house without gardens or paths or miracles. I live in a house which is protected from the knives of the street by snails, birds and incantations. I live in a house which shudders with the praise songs of passing cars filled with sunglasses and guns and sperm. I live in a house which lures dappled shade to its front rooms every morning while heat drools through the back but each afternoon the roles reverse. I live in a house which stays sane only because the sun can move. I live in a house whose neighbours are neon and perpetual complacency. I live in a house where every day the doors and windows open a little wider to allow wind to blow in between its walls. I live in a house with foundations still brooding for the tonguestrokes of the sea. I live in a house which rocks in sorrow with its memories of spurned beggars and unconsoled children. I live in a house which is slowly becoming my body.

VI

Old flames

*If you reject perfection in order
to turn to the quotidian, where
does desire get its image?*
— Joan Metelerkamp

1

The children that you hold
beside you, one on your back,
the other loosely by the arm,
appear no burden at all
though there are no rainbows
to shine upon their faces
held up expectantly
                    except
the glinting of artificial light
reflected off endless shop windows
enticing and vaunted as
shipwrecks.

          For them
you sang your body open
a sustaining host of bread
from which they dropped,
soft skins and the impulse
to be loved, with already
hardening crusts, into time.

Your semblance will flow
across their features
then disappear
                into the oversight
of no one's chronicle

and you begin to wonder
why what begins as love
freely offered
         resolves
to patience or neglect

when it is too late

an old lady frail with your fury
in the sunshine.

    2

You write: I wish you could meet
              the kids. They are starting
              to bud into real little people.
              Emilia's learnt to colour in
              with crayons, and Eryn asks
              unanswerable questions
              all the time it drives me
              mad

I write: poor little shits. How will
              they survive? It's all
              money and status out there
              these days

You write: and birth! It was exactly
              like being prised open on a vice.
              I'd already felt like soggy dough
              for nine months, and didn't realise
              it just got worse

I write: big deal. What makes it so compelling
              to keep *your* genes eternal?
                      And forget
              the motherhood thing. How are you?

You write: shit, you're kind of out of it!
And, besides, what gives
you the right to criticize?
You never have acknowledged
that I can be tender and serene.
I don't abandon people

I write: huh?

You write: during the small hours here
next to me Wayne stirs in his sleep,
cries out only until I lay
an arm across his body

               whisper

   Yes, sssh, be quiet, love;
   I am here. I am still here

I write: so, Mother Theresa …
what's *he* got on his conscience?

You write: at least he's better than that
morose second-rate accountant
who was my first husband
… and why can't *you* keep
a relationship, Peter Pan?
You never were an expert
in how to be attentive

I write: that's not true. Remember
that first afternoon slipping
your shoulder slipping
against my hand

             the freckles

powdering your back? I

You write: ja. I thought you were
an unlovable pimply boy
but then you danced
crazy high with delight
maybe on something

You write: next to the campfire
where the place was
stenched-out with pine

I write: and the smell of sweat!
I never dreamed a woman
could have kiss curls
down there

You write: … we should stop this.
I don't love you anymore

I write: and me, neither
– but you were nuts
to go get married *again*

You write: (silence)

I write: I'm sick of what you
dare not think

You write: and *I'm* sick of you
speculating about all the things
you dare not do

3

It's all or nothing for me these days
and so I seem indifferent.

I'm entitled by that nobody
who wants me to forget his name
when explaining myself to the guards
that brag along the borders
                              left in place
when we withdrew to these
                              farflung regimes
where we now hide behind our faces.

I find I can read your letters
only in waiting rooms, or
                    in the deep
secret corners of that final hour before the sun
when dogs alone remain alert
to know they're inconsolable.

So it's our choice now
to grow frivolous at funerals, aware
the blood still moans and flirts
insinuates its tongue in and out the heart

that urge we once called passion.

    4

If you can imagine
a child-mind
that still has faith

its island of self
peopled
        and awash
    awash
with possibility

then you can surely
remember who you are
when you were

       where

do men, women take
their cherishing, their need?

I don't know.
       All I know is

there is something needs to be done with this,
       though not by us.
The rivers have wavered into drought for too long.
A young girl perhaps your daughter ponders
stands staring out over a legacy of dust as night comes on
hesitates
       and thinks of the ocean.

Coitus

She has plunged her hands with mine
into that resonant space of night
where the spider weaves patiently
its mystery of enclosure

and lies under me
with nipples firm as darkening grapes,
thighs a fork of desire and forgetfulness,
as if she were contented.

Now she holds in her first hand
the swelling pledge of her womb,
                              the other,
a tinkling necklace of crumbled bones.

Our bodies forming are the spider.

I like

Marx the visionary, crumbs in his beard, armpits stinking,
    hard-working, belching food –
                        prophet for the whole
    grey kaleidoscope of lives eked out in kitchens
            on assembly lines at looms at furnaces
            perceiver of the splintered mirror
                    of our isolate repressions,
            abuser of women, fractured himself –
Tathagata the foe of adipose theories, scientist
            of a single flower bending
                in the wind, saying
        How can you liberate others when you can't
    even recognise your own hand in front of your face?
            Displaying a swift abhya mudra to intellectuals
                rapt in their own egos –
Zappa the gravel-voiced, thumbing his nose at the outraged,
        those who would crimp human waywardness and joyous noise
            into the solemn musics of assumption and
                amnesia
                        whose death still buzzes
        like a fly through their chaste and chastised harmonies,
            their television videos hip-hopping from one
                coinage to another!
The ten fingers of Cecil Taylor leaping salmon-bright
                up a waterfall
            of black and white keys, the sharp
        flats, founding buildings of sound
                tap-tapping towards new edifices
    on eighty-eight tuned drums ...

and if these days

      my stereo's malfunctioning
      music is anaemic from the sweet breath of pixels
      on its jugular
      my bookcase has toppled over
      from an overweight of statement
      and enlightenment is impossible
      in this city of industrial waste
                    where the sky's fletched always
                with feathers of acid orange
                       where pollution
         stirs its daily soup
       and tyres fawn at increasing speeds
to ever smoother highways
             where bureaucrat after bureaucrat
         brushes each dawn hisher smile afresh
            to find new ways
                  to leach taxes
        to produce haemophilic captour sunsets

who gives a shit for them

so what we've not had a thought all afternoon so what
            it's become too dark to read
     and still too light to drowse
         so what

listen smell taste touch see

branches swaying with pears
  globose and bird-pecked peer
    knock through a cracked window –
        perfumes riot above their vase –
      trains toting skirts and trousers
clank back and forth in steely frustration
          beyond the fences
    of cold rain-fudged backyards:
the cicada voices of children
          in the street
    quarrel in honest language
            with scant knowledge
        of the phrases the false gifts
  of words they will one day use
      to wrap up adult guilt

gnaw these worlds
    inhale their colours
      feel your hair
        bristle
            with unplumbed sound

your hand a parenthesis reaching out to me
stirs me now
      and,
      emphatically,
          at times like these anew
          what I like best
      is you

Your smile is a sudden bird

Your smile is a sudden bird
alighting on your face. Bushes shake:
my eyes open: the usual morning
blears into its existence
of car alarms and smog,
and then, you are.

                     There. With me

decisive as a heron
dipping one leg with forethought
into troubled shallows, seeking –
or a warbler's cry unknown
within thick sedge,
shy inside its tiny frame
but confident in song –

in a manner of speaking only

– for you soon grow tired
of the fumbled maleness
of all metaphor
            tell me
huh! I'm this natural world
of birds 'n shit no more
than you are, buddy!

– but as my universe
is stirred from sleep
how can I
how can I explain

the joy upwelling in my mind
anticipating your presence
except as a prospect
of bustling birds I
wait each day to see?

Can you remember once

under a towering african holly
spread out dense around us
next to a river easing slow
between two krantzes a forest
inverted in its reluctant mirror
we sat, expecting nothing,
talked of what was important
only to us

        then heard
a sound of creaking doors
a *kok, kok, kok* an everywhere
of rustling of cavorting
as eight – nine! – louries
came prancing all at once
up and down the branches
of our chosen tree
ignoring us, and we

knew them
a crown of green and red,
birdtree upon our love, a motion
of fugitive life immeasurable
and endless, benison
more blessed

because we were surprised?

So words can be made possible
both to them, and you
woman of flesh and blood;
with you

it is my luck
to live beneath a wind-filled sky
with death a freight of clouds that looms
merely to etch your gestures, voice,
your moods

my face uprisen
as you call our love to flight –

knowing you have within your palms
perpetually new birds.

Stonework

there are wings do not unfold for flight –
the mind is a perilous grey stone
carved to no need!

the weight (to my hand) invents
love a stone already aloft
and departing,
     by the mind's wings
the chisel's wounding strokes borne,
never alighting,

tossed differently
to what was intended,
while around it the sky alters.

VII

Death of a poet

Between the edges
of his sight
a rusted mattock leans:
a clod of soil,
turned long ago, utters anew
its hopeful stalk
of grass.

Bees whisper
in their warming hives.
          Spring peers out.
The sky ages golden,
slab of stolen honey.

His chair
no longer creaks;
head bent forward
as though listening
to his navel,

he is falling asleep,
old man, asleep, he is
falling

a tiny flycatcher
hawks from a branch
above him
– snaps its beak –
flies down. Flies back.
Flies down.

The betrayal of narrative

And my friends die, one by one,
each caught in accidental amber
like a fly
            within the gelled memory
of a various summer I have concocted.

The first fell from heaven
a flaming comet
                then was
quenched. His ribcage now
is lighter than the sky he loved,
lies deeper than all knowledge –
tides gently back and forth
                            a lair
in which small fish can sleep secure.

The second flopped and bled from the mouth
on a pavement unyielding as surprise
in front of the door he'd thought was home
before fourteen holes to lung and stomach
and an assassin's footsteps fading
taught him another
                    more urgent destination.

Here my poem trips on stone.
My poem must stop short.
It has a swollen ankle.

The third spoke at the end in whispers
despite the voice I'd loved
conversing through noon forests
which could blast birds from their nests
or dangle the pompous from its utterance.
He became in time less
                            discernible than grass,
organs prodded to new shapes
by the tumour of each day passing
and vomit his chief mode of speech
until he longed for death,
                    a comrade
to stride alongside him
and say nothing.

My poem trips on stone.
It can't move forward, or start back,
but loathes this standing still.
It gives nothing to the hole in the air
        waiting here right next to me
each friend has learnt to be.

It is a trifle to condescend
to a corpse that's not one's own
with words. Which is in turn
impossible. I write this, then,

to staunch my coming silence
before it cannot matter; trail
the unruly tips to my fingers
through the ink

of this grudging autumn morning
dried hot now on my face alone

the space
beyond this poem cawing with sorrow,
my heart
still wild
as a crow inside me.

Black lizard on a white rock

Left flank

pulses: your tiny
heart.

Alive,
knowing no safe

resting place.

The crossing

no more feigning speech   i'm caught out in the open
nothing to write down   peer up where unfolding
silence fleers mists all around   then bares cheeks of high crag
what can loquacity achieve here   so posed so unconsoling

you're like us who am i   we're the mimics of men
women draped in drab cities   where we labour to train
for carnivals of false homage   to our identities to a history
which our ancestors only felt as   minds and bodies in pain

the initiates stood and watched me   puzzled this morning
they kept their place counting   each pace away with their eyes
blobs in faces daubed white   with ochre they had told me
their forefathers' myths much like mine   nothing new mostly lies

shown their route down to a swamp   land of pride sticky as tar
palsied with violence   broadcasting self-renown
i left them wrapt in the cloying   warm skins of their stories
a tremor in my limbs climbing   each time i glanced down

a dead tree flung down   its most ponderous branch
in front of me grass hissed   near the edge of my sight
baboons bickered and mocked   at each other's foreheads
but i'm safer here now where   just the hungry will bite

reached a time when old age   merely quickens me further
to find biographies that fit   hearts not yet in defeat
vault a final stream's sanctuary   its blonde blazons of rubble
i stumble on up the thighs   of a poort in fat heat

the sun hangs sluggish   grape of the sky's dried-up vine
while proteas blacken   no soil settles for seed
i search for peopled valleys   omened sprouting with promise
where a community of laughter   gives in concord with need

but lost still in these doldrums of self   pity and anger
those who walked through this space   before me are gone
no path but their spoor of   futile tears shed at random
i can tell you there's ash   here but little birdsong

i can tell you the terms used   to fix meaning have vanished
i trudge on with my patience on   stonerims thin as a vase
i live with the memory   that once i had knowledge
but once or twice at night here   i have made out new stars

The slow war of the flea

… as long as we have faith, we have no hope.
To hope, we have to break *the faith.*
– Arundhati Roy

1

on the contrary
i am not ready to leave
even at the end of the dry season,
when the homes of larks and spiders
flare up and burn like museums,
as i plant bergamot in the wrong climate
in a hope of future bees
               and the stars
drip their milk from the bottle of the galaxy
night after night

            – where is your land, my brother
my sister who contend through voices
to find your own, where are your people –
pursuing speech to make a world alive to sharing
as you wage against the powerful
your slow war of the flea

wherever you decide to go from here
goseame i'll come with you
but you'll have to take me as i am
voetstoots

2

now that the detonations of bombs have ended
their pontificating and we can think to stop
picking shrapnel from our flesh and psyches
and go

about the absent-minded tasks of daily living
i find
     there is some force that tickles
the air as it evacuates my mouth,
so that my gossip giggles
          yes i tell you this

you who have kept your truth,
who do not heed the reversals of a mirror,
who know what it is in the middle of calamity
to feel unprompted a fierce jubilation

i only ask this minute
to defend my shadow, to drop my shoes
and apply cleansing sand and water
to the miles that clog my feet,
the history my soles have trodden
          i am

so bewildered in these warrens
of hoarded wealth and foregone conclusions,
the stale boardroom musings of those
who accumulate backwards
dung beetles

i say their cites have an edge
their pantomimes will have finale –
take my hand so i may go
further. There is no other secret:

we are always only one choice
       away

       from
an impenetrable gift, a politics
of the focused eye: a place

where our bodies
may move in rhythm
with the dawn.

VIII

The dream of the cricket

sing for your own reasons
or merely to disturb
the molecules of oxygen

sing to please yourself
or call them call call call
to them who couldn't
give a damn

sing since to be lent
the conceit of a voice
seems to its celebrant
a minor miracle

– but here you are alone
enthusiast of echoes

– here it is quite useless
to conjure wing-cased words
that hop but long to fly

– here there is a massacre
that waits for you for me

who cares find magic
you who proffers portents
from each doleful place

from within the crannies
each rub arub
all over in the air

134

a gift
a tiny miracle

flushed from cover
given the boot
betrayed always
by your song ...

a *mmmrrr* a *ccclll!*

a*mmrracclllll!*

The undergrowth

I call the tchagra from dense thickets
the ponderous glide
the sly purr of hidden wings
between branch-syllables

if it sleeps at night
its eyes stay wide open
and its eggs glimmer anxious candles
it tricks the shouting crickets their rhetoric
towards its beak
                it knows
that all song is a struggle with trepidation
there is always a sea near its hunger

fists of light thrash the weary beach like a bandit
fledglings topple from their nest in aspiration
and are misbegotten they dwindle
useless plucked corpses

dawn swaggering up from the sand
clones itself from bush to bush
ignites the diligence of spiders
the sun's yolk dribbles from its clasp
the sea sniggers again in boredom

the yolk of each letter spurts away from its word
no longer to be spoken
eggshells scrunch and sough along the dunes
get lost in wrack and leaf litter

how to describe this life lived
in the labyrinths between the seconds
I want no bird in the hand

I wait for the tchagra to fly

The dream of the amnesic gatekeeper

1

As one who's been used
all his life to sheep and goats. And always

a traveller, then another,
struggling your way down the hill
towards me, towards my fences,
usually in misery.

Sometimes I spoke to you

before demanding your allegiance
to the ones we called our masters;
watched you then proceed on the half-attentive
compulsions of your daily lives
into the distance

until I found a dream which told me
my judgments were no more acute than yours,
and what's more

all the things I did
belied the man I said I was.

So I came to juggle the feelings
I thought I possessed, lost my grip,
and my heart like an egg shattered
on the floor of the habitual tired battles
of myself and everyone.

To my bafflement I only laughed.

Now I live
secret as a cobra in dry grass,

I am so tired
of your fixed resolve, your proud acts
of presuming on each dawn.

    2

All of you remote secure in the bastions
of your heatsapped souls listen to me —

if you want to visit me
here where I farm words in an endless wind
with blisters on my thoughts and thumbs
what can I say

you'll find the road
between the desert and the sea
— always too little or too much —
deceived by mist imminent with rockfall
between the wetlands and the mountains
of the moon
                known
neither to toad nor buzzard

here I keep no dogs
the gate is wide open
all my locks are rusted
there is no number on the fence
no name to this street
where truth tempts blind children.

I may be here to greet you,
if you come.